The Chaperon

Henry James

1st WORLD
LIBRARY
Literary Society

The Chaperon

Henry James

© 1st World Library – Literary Society, 2004
PO Box 2211
Fairfield, IA 52556
www.1stworldlibrary.org
First Edition

LCCN: 2004091201

Softcover ISBN: 1-59540-647-6
eBook ISBN: 1-59540-747-2

Purchase *"The Chaperon"*
as a traditional bound book at:
www.1stWorldLibrary.org/purchase.asp?ISBN=1-59540-647-6

1st World Library Literary Society is a nonprofit organization dedicated to promoting literacy by:

- Creating a free internet library accessible from any computer worldwide.
- Hosting writing competitions and offering book publishing scholarships.

Readers interested in supporting literacy through sponsorship, donations or membership please contact:
literacy@1stworldlibrary.org
Check us out at: www.1stworldlibrary.org

The Chaperon
contributed by the Charles Family
in support of
1st World Library Literary Society

CHAPTER I.

An old lady, in a high drawing-room, had had her chair moved close to the fire, where she sat knitting and warming her knees. She was dressed in deep mourning; her face had a faded nobleness, tempered, however, by the somewhat illiberal compression assumed by her lips in obedience to something that was passing in her mind. She was far from the lamp, but though her eyes were fixed upon her active needles she was not looking at them. What she really saw was quite another train of affairs. The room was spacious and dim; the thick London fog had oozed into it even through its superior defences. It was full of dusky, massive, valuable things. The old lady sat motionless save for the regularity of her clicking needles, which seemed as personal to her and as expressive as prolonged fingers. If she was thinking something out, she was thinking it thoroughly.

When she looked up, on the entrance of a girl of twenty, it might have been guessed that the appearance of this young lady was not an interruption of her meditation, but rather a contribution to it. The young lady, who was charming to behold, was also in deep mourning, which had a freshness, if mourning can be fresh, an air of having been lately put on. She went straight to the bell beside the chimney-piece and pulled it, while in her other hand she held a sealed and directed letter. Her companion glanced in silence at the letter; then she looked still harder at her work. The girl hovered near the fireplace, without speaking, and after a due, a dignified interval the butler appeared in response to the bell. The time had been sufficient to make the silence between the ladies seem long. The younger one asked the butler to see that her letter should be posted; and after he had gone out she moved vaguely about the room, as if to give her grandmother - for such was the elder personage - a chance to begin a colloquy of which she herself preferred not to strike the first note. As equally with herself her companion was on the face of it capable of holding out, the tension, though it was already late in the evening, might have lasted long. But the old lady after a little appeared to recognise, a trifle ungraciously, the girl's superior resources.

"Have you written to your mother?"

"Yes, but only a few lines, to tell her I shall come and see her in the morning."

"Is that all you've got to say?" asked the grandmother.

"I don't quite know what you want me to say."

"I want you to say that you've made up your mind."

"Yes, I've done that, granny."

"You intend to respect your father's wishes?"

"It depends upon what you mean by respecting them. I do justice to the feelings by which they were dictated."

Henry James

"What do you mean by justice?" the old lady retorted.

The girl was silent a moment; then she said: "You'll see my idea of it."

"I see it already! You'll go and live with her."

"I shall talk the situation over with her to-morrow and tell her that I think that will be best."

"Best for her, no doubt!"

"What's best for her is best for me."

"And for your brother and sister?" As the girl made no reply to this her grandmother went on: "What's best for them is that you should acknowledge some responsibility in regard to them and, considering how young they are, try and do something for them."

"They must do as I've done - they must act for themselves. They have their means now, and they're free."

"Free? They're mere children."

"Let me remind you that Eric is older than I."

"He doesn't like his mother," said the old lady, as if that were an answer.

"I never said he did. And she adores him."

"Oh, your mother's adorations!"

"Don't abuse her now," the girl rejoined, after a pause.

The old lady forbore to abuse her, but she made up for it the next moment by saying: "It will be dreadful for Edith."

"What will be dreadful?"

"Your desertion of her."

"The desertion's on her side."

"Her consideration for her father does her honour."

"Of course I'm a brute, n'en parlons plus," said the girl. "We must go our respective ways," she added, in a tone of extreme wisdom and philosophy.

Her grandmother straightened out her knitting and began to roll it up. "Be so good as to ring for my maid," she said, after a minute. The young lady rang, and there was another wait and another conscious hush. Before the maid came her mistress remarked: "Of course then you'll not come to ME, you know."

"What do you mean by 'coming' to you?"

"I can't receive you on that footing."

"She'll not come WITH me, if you mean that."

"I don't mean that," said the old lady, getting up as her maid came in. This attendant took her work from her, gave her an arm and helped her out of the room, while Rose Tramore, standing before the fire and looking into it, faced the idea that her grandmother's door would now under all circumstances be closed to her. She lost no time however in brooding over this anomaly: it only added energy to her determination to act. All she could do to-night was to go to bed, for she felt utterly weary. She had been living, in imagination, in a prospective struggle, and it had left her as exhausted as a real fight. Moreover this was the culmination of a crisis, of weeks of suspense, of a long, hard strain. Her father had been laid in his grave five days before, and that morning his will had been read. In the afternoon she had got Edith off to St. Leonard's with their aunt Julia, and then she had had a wretched talk with Eric. Lastly, she had made up her mind to act in opposition to the formidable will, to a clause which embodied if not exactly a provision, a recommendation singularly emphatic. She went to bed and slept the sleep of the just.

"Oh, my dear, how charming! I must take another house!" It was in these words that her mother responded to the announcement Rose had just formally made and with which she had vaguely expected to produce a certain dignity of effect. In the way of emotion there was apparently no effect at all, and the girl was wise enough to know that this was not simply on account of the general line of non-allusion taken by the extremely pretty woman before her, who looked like her elder sister. Mrs. Tramore had never manifested, to her daughter, the slightest consciousness that her position was peculiar; but the recollection of something more than that fine policy was required to explain such a failure, to appreciate Rose's sacrifice. It was simply a fresh reminder that she had never appreciated anything, that she was nothing but a tinted and stippled surface. Her situation was peculiar indeed. She had been the heroine of a scandal which had grown dim only because, in the eyes of the London world, it paled in the lurid light of the contemporaneous. That attention had been fixed on it for several days, fifteen years before; there had been a high relish of the vivid evidence as to his wife's misconduct with which, in the divorce-court, Charles Tramore had judged well to regale a cynical public. The case was pronounced awfully bad, and he obtained his decree. The folly of the wife had been inconceivable, in spite of other examples: she had quitted her children, she had followed the "other fellow" abroad. The other fellow hadn't married her, not having had time: he had lost his life in the Mediterranean by the capsizing of a boat, before the prohibitory term had expired.

Mrs. Tramore had striven to extract from this accident something of the austerity of widowhood; but her mourning only made her deviation more public, she was a widow whose husband was awkwardly alive. She had not prowled about the Continent on the classic lines; she had come back to London to take her chance. But London would give her no chance, would have nothing to say to her; as many persons had remarked, you could never tell how London would behave. It would not receive Mrs. Tramore again on any terms, and when she was spoken of, which now was not often, it was inveterately said of her that she went nowhere. Apparently she had not the qualities for which London compounds; though in the cases in which it does compound you may often wonder what these qualities are. She had not at any rate been successful: her lover was dead, her husband was liked and her children were pitied, for in payment for a topic London will parenthetically pity. It was thought interesting and magnanimous that Charles Tramore had not married again. The disadvantage to his children of the miserable story was thus left uncorrected, and this, rather oddly, was counted as HIS sacrifice. His mother, whose arrangements were elaborate, looked after them a great deal, and they enjoyed a mixture of laxity and discipline under the roof of their aunt, Miss Tramore, who was independent, having, for reasons that the two ladies had exhaustively discussed, determined to lead her own

life. She had set up a home at St. Leonard's, and that contracted shore had played a considerable part in the upbringing of the little Tramores. They knew about their mother, as the phrase was, but they didn't know her; which was naturally deemed more pathetic for them than for her. She had a house in Chester Square and an income and a victoria - it served all purposes, as she never went out in the evening - and flowers on her window-sills, and a remarkable appearance of youth. The income was supposed to be in part the result of a bequest from the man for whose sake she had committed the error of her life, and in the appearance of youth there was a slightly impertinent implication that it was a sort of afterglow of the same connection.

Her children, as they grew older, fortunately showed signs of some individuality of disposition. Edith, the second girl, clung to her aunt Julia; Eric, the son, clung frantically to polo; while Rose, the elder daughter, appeared to cling mainly to herself. Collectively, of course, they clung to their father, whose attitude in the family group, however, was casual and intermittent. He was charming and vague; he was like a clever actor who often didn't come to rehearsal. Fortune, which but for that one stroke had been generous to him, had provided him with deputies and trouble-takers, as well as with whimsical opinions, and a reputation for excellent taste, and whist at his club, and perpetual cigars on morocco sofas, and a beautiful absence of purpose. Nature had thrown in a remarkably fine hand, which he sometimes passed over his children's heads when they were glossy from the nursery brush. On Rose's eighteenth birthday he said to her that she might go to see her mother, on condition that her visits should be limited to an hour each time and to four in the year. She was to go alone; the other children were not included in the arrangement. This was the result of a visit that he himself had paid his repudiated wife at her urgent request, their only encounter during the fifteen years. The girl knew as much as this from her aunt Julia, who was full of tell-tale secrecies. She availed herself eagerly of the license, and in course of the period that elapsed before her father's death she spent with Mrs. Tramore exactly eight hours by the watch. Her father, who was as inconsistent and disappointing as he was amiable, spoke to her of her mother only once afterwards. This occasion had been the sequel of her first visit, and he had made no use of it to ask what she thought of the personality in Chester Square or how she liked it. He had only said "Did she take you out?" and when Rose answered "Yes, she put me straight into a carriage and drove me up and down Bond Street," had rejoined sharply "See that that never occurs again." It never did, but once was enough, every one they knew having happened to be in Bond Street at that particular hour.

After this the periodical interview took place in private, in Mrs. Tramore's beautiful little wasted drawing-room. Rose knew that, rare as these occasions were, her mother would not have kept her "all to herself" had there been anybody she could have shown her to. But in the poor lady's social void there was no one; she had after all her own correctness and she consistently preferred isolation to inferior contacts. So

Henry James

her daughter was subjected only to the maternal; it was not necessary to be definite in qualifying that. The girl had by this time a collection of ideas, gathered by impenetrable processes; she had tasted, in the ostracism of her ambiguous parent, of the acrid fruit of the tree of knowledge. She not only had an approximate vision of what every one had done, but she had a private judgment for each case. She had a particular vision of her father, which did not interfere with his being dear to her, but which was directly concerned in her resolution, after his death, to do the special thing he had expressed the wish she should not do. In the general estimate her grandmother and her grandmother's money had their place, and the strong probability that any enjoyment of the latter commodity would now be withheld from her. It included Edith's marked inclination to receive the law, and doubtless eventually a more substantial memento, from Miss Tramore, and opened the question whether her own course might not contribute to make her sister's appear heartless. The answer to this question however would depend on the success that might attend her own, which would very possibly be small. Eric's attitude was eminently simple; he didn't care to know people who didn't know HIS people. If his mother should ever get back into society perhaps he would take her up. Rose Tramore had decided to do what she could to bring this consummation about; and strangely enough - so mixed were her superstitions and her heresies - a large part of her motive lay in the value she attached to such a consecration.

Of her mother intrinsically she thought very little now, and if her eyes were fixed on a special achievement it was much more for the sake of that achievement and to satisfy a latent energy that was in her than because her heart was wrung by this sufferer. Her heart had not been wrung at all, though she had quite held it out for the experience. Her purpose was a pious game, but it was still essentially a game. Among the ideas I have mentioned she had her idea of triumph. She had caught the inevitable note, the pitch, on her very first visit to Chester Square. She had arrived there in intense excitement, and her excitement was left on her hands in a manner that reminded her of a difficult air she had once heard sung at the opera when no one applauded the performer. That flatness had made her sick, and so did this, in another way. A part of her agitation proceeded from the fact that her aunt Julia had told her, in the manner of a burst of confidence, something she was not to repeat, that she was in appearance the very image of the lady in Chester Square. The motive that prompted this declaration was between aunt Julia and her conscience; but it was a great emotion to the girl to find her entertainer so beautiful. She was tall and exquisitely slim; she had hair more exactly to Rose Tramore's taste than any other she had ever seen, even to every detail in the way it was dressed, and a complexion and a figure of the kind that are always spoken of as "lovely." Her eyes were irresistible, and so were her clothes, though the clothes were perhaps a little more precisely the right thing than the eyes. Her appearance was marked to her daughter's sense by the highest distinction; though it may be mentioned that this had never been the opinion of all the world. It was a revelation to Rose that she herself might look a little like that. She knew however that aunt Julia had not seen her deposed sister-in-law for a long time, and she had a general impression that Mrs. Tramore was to-day a more complete production - for instance as regarded her air of youth - than she had ever been. There was no excitement on her side - that was all her visitor's; there

Henry James

was no emotion - that was excluded by the plan, to say nothing of conditions more primal. Rose had from the first a glimpse of her mother's plan. It was to mention nothing and imply nothing, neither to acknowledge, to explain nor to extenuate. She would leave everything to her child; with her child she was secure. She only wanted to get back into society; she would leave even that to her child, whom she treated not as a high-strung and heroic daughter, a creature of exaltation, of devotion, but as a new, charming, clever, useful friend, a little younger than herself. Already on that first day she had talked about dressmakers. Of course, poor thing, it was to be remembered that in her circumstances there were not many things she COULD talk about. "She wants to go out again; that's the only thing in the wide world she wants," Rose had promptly, compendiously said to herself. There had been a sequel to this observation, uttered, in intense engrossment, in her own room half an hour before she had, on the important evening, made known her decision to her grandmother: "Then I'll TAKE her out!"

"She'll drag you down, she'll drag you down!" Julia Tramore permitted herself to remark to her niece, the next day, in a tone of feverish prophecy.

As the girl's own theory was that all the dragging there might be would be upward, and moreover administered by herself, she could look at her aunt with a cold and inscrutable eye.

"Very well, then, I shall be out of your sight, from the pinnacle you occupy, and I sha'n't trouble you."

"Do you reproach me for my disinterested exertions, for the way I've toiled over you, the way I've lived for you?" Miss Tramore demanded.

"Don't reproach ME for being kind to my mother and I won't reproach you for anything."

"She'll keep you out of everything - she'll make you miss everything," Miss Tramore continued.

"Then she'll make me miss a great deal that's odious," said the girl.

"You're too young for such extravagances," her aunt declared.

"And yet Edith, who is younger than I, seems to be too old for them: how do you arrange that? My mother's society will make me older," Rose replied.

"Don't speak to me of your mother; you HAVE no mother."

"Then if I'm an orphan I must settle things for myself."

"Do you justify her, do you approve of her?" cried Miss Tramore, who was inferior to her niece in capacity for retort and whose limitations made the girl appear pert.

Rose looked at her a moment in silence; then she said, turning away: "I think she's charming."

"And do you propose to become charming in the same manner?"

"Her manner is perfect; it would be an excellent model. But I can't discuss my mother with you."

"You'll have to discuss her with some other people!" Miss Tramore proclaimed, going out of the room.

Rose wondered whether this were a general or a particular vaticination. There was something her aunt might have meant by it, but her aunt rarely meant the best thing she might have meant. Miss Tramore had come up from St. Leonard's in response to a telegram from her own parent, for an occasion like the present brought with it, for a few hours, a certain relaxation of their dissent. "Do what you can to stop her," the old lady had said; but her daughter found that the most she could do was not much. They both had a baffled sense that Rose had thought the question out a good deal further than they; and this was particularly irritating to Mrs. Tramore, as consciously the cleverer of the two. A question thought out as far as SHE could think it had always appeared to her to have performed its human uses; she had never encountered a ghost emerging from that extinction. Their great contention was that Rose would cut herself off; and certainly if she wasn't afraid of that she wasn't afraid of anything. Julia Tramore could only tell her mother how little the girl was afraid. She was already prepared to leave the house, taking with her the possessions, or her share of them, that had accumulated there during her father's illness. There had been a going and coming of her maid, a thumping about of boxes, an ordering of four-wheelers; it appeared to old Mrs. Tramore that something of the objectionableness, the indecency, of her granddaughter's prospective connection had already gathered about the place. It was a violation of the decorum of bereavement which was still fresh there, and from the indignant gloom of the mistress of the house you might have inferred not so much that the daughter was about to depart as that the mother was about to arrive. There had been no conversation on the dreadful subject at luncheon; for at luncheon at Mrs. Tramore's (her son never came to it) there were always, even after funerals and other miseries, stray guests of both sexes whose policy it was to be cheerful and superficial. Rose had sat down as if nothing had happened - nothing worse, that is, than her father's death; but no one had spoken of anything that any one else was thinking of.

Before she left the house a servant brought her a message from her grandmother - the old lady desired to see her in the drawing-room. She had on her bonnet, and she went down as if she were about to step into her cab. Mrs. Tramore sat there with her eternal knitting, from which she forebore even to raise her eyes as, after a silence that seemed to express the fulness of her reprobation, while Rose stood motionless, she began: "I wonder if you really understand what you're doing."

"I think so. I'm not so stupid."

"I never thought you were; but I don't know what to make of you now. You're giving up everything."

The girl was tempted to inquire whether her grand-mother called herself "everything"; but she checked this question, answering instead that she knew she was giving up much.

"You're taking a step of which you will feel the effect to the end of your days," Mrs. Tramore went on.

"In a good conscience, I heartily hope," said Rose.

"Your father's conscience was good enough for his

mother; it ought to be good enough for his daughter."

Rose sat down - she could afford to - as if she wished to be very attentive and were still accessible to argument. But this demonstration only ushered in, after a moment, the surprising words "I don't think papa had any conscience."

"What in the name of all that's unnatural do you mean?" Mrs. Tramore cried, over her glasses. "The dearest and best creature that ever lived!"

"He was kind, he had charming impulses, he was delightful. But he never reflected."

Mrs. Tramore stared, as if at a language she had never heard, a farrago, a galimatias. Her life was made up of items, but she had never had to deal, intellectually, with a fine shade. Then while her needles, which had paused an instant, began to fly again, she rejoined: "Do you know what you are, my dear? You're a dreadful little prig. Where do you pick up such talk?"

"Of course I don't mean to judge between them," Rose pursued. "I can only judge between my mother and myself. Papa couldn't judge for me." And with this she got up.

"One would think you were horrid. I never thought so before."

"Thank you for that."

"You're embarking on a struggle with society," continued Mrs. Tramore, indulging in an unusual flight of oratory. "Society will put you in your place."

"Hasn't it too many other things to do?" asked the girl.

This question had an ingenuity which led her grand-mother to meet it with a merely provisional and somewhat sketchy answer. "Your ignorance would be melancholy if your behaviour were not so insane."

"Oh, no; I know perfectly what she'll do!" Rose replied, almost gaily. "She'll drag me down."

"She won't even do that," the old lady declared contradictiously. "She'll keep you forever in the same dull hole."

"I shall come and see YOU, granny, when I want something more lively."

"You may come if you like, but you'll come no further than the door. If you leave this house now you don't enter it again."

Rose hesitated a moment. "Do you really mean that?"

"You may judge whether I choose such a time to joke."

"Good-bye, then," said the girl.

"Good-bye."

Rose quitted the room successfully enough; but on the other side of the door, on the landing, she sank into a chair and buried her face in her hands. She had burst into tears, and she sobbed there for a moment, trying hard to recover herself, so as to go downstairs without showing any traces of emotion, passing before the servants and again perhaps before aunt Julia. Mrs.

Tramore was too old to cry; she could only drop her knitting and, for a long time, sit with her head bowed and her eyes closed.

Rose had reckoned justly with her aunt Julia; there were no footmen, but this vigilant virgin was posted at the foot of the stairs. She offered no challenge however; she only said: "There's some one in the parlour who wants to see you." The girl demanded a name, but Miss Tramore only mouthed inaudibly and winked and waved. Rose instantly reflected that there was only one man in the world her aunt would look such deep things about. "Captain Jay?" her own eyes asked, while Miss Tramore's were those of a conspirator: they were, for a moment, the only embarrassed eyes Rose had encountered that day. They contributed to make aunt Julia's further response evasive, after her niece inquired if she had communicated in advance with this visitor. Miss Tramore merely said that he had been upstairs with her mother - hadn't she mentioned it? - and had been waiting for her. She thought herself acute in not putting the question of the girl's seeing him before her as a favour to him or to herself; she presented it as a duty, and wound up with the proposition: "It's not fair to him, it's not kind, not to let him speak to you before you go."

"What does he want to say?" Rose demanded.

"Go in and find out."

She really knew, for she had found out before; but after standing uncertain an instant she went in. "The parlour" was the name that had always been borne by a spacious sitting-room downstairs, an apartment occupied by her father during his frequent phases of residence in Hill Street - episodes increasingly frequent after his house in the country had, in consequence, as Rose perfectly knew, of his spending too much money, been disposed of at a sacrifice which he always characterised as horrid. He had been left with the place in Hertfordshire and his mother with the London house, on the general understanding that they would change about; but during the last years the community had grown more rigid, mainly at his mother's expense. The parlour was full of his memory and his habits and his things - his books and pictures and bibelots, objects that belonged now to Eric. Rose had sat in it for hours since his death; it was the place in which she could still be nearest to him. But she felt far from him as Captain Jay rose erect on her opening the door. This was a very different presence. He had not liked Captain Jay. She herself had, but not enough to make a great complication of her father's coldness. This afternoon however she foresaw complications. At the very outset for instance she was not pleased with his having arranged such a surprise for her with her grandmother and her aunt. It was probably aunt Julia who had sent for him; her grandmother wouldn't have done it. It placed him immediately on their side, and Rose was almost as disappointed at this as if she had not known it was quite where he would naturally be. He had never paid her a special visit, but if that was what he wished to do why shouldn't he have waited till she should be under her mother's roof? She knew the reason, but she had an angry prospect of enjoyment in making him express it. She liked him enough, after all, if it were measured by the idea of what she could make him do.

In Bertram Jay the elements were surprisingly mingled; you would have gone astray, in reading him, if you had counted on finding the complements of

Henry James

some of his qualities. He would not however have struck you in the least as incomplete, for in every case in which you didn't find the complement you would have found the contradiction. He was in the Royal Engineers, and was tall, lean and high-shouldered. He looked every inch a soldier, yet there were people who considered that he had missed his vocation in not becoming a parson. He took a public interest in the spiritual life of the army. Other persons still, on closer observation, would have felt that his most appropriate field was neither the army nor the church, but simply the world - the social, successful, worldly world. If he had a sword in one hand and a Bible in the other he had a Court Guide concealed somewhere about his person. His profile was hard and handsome, his eyes were both cold and kind, his dark straight hair was imperturbably smooth and prematurely streaked with grey. There was nothing in existence that he didn't take seriously. He had a first-rate power of work and an ambition as minutely organised as a German plan of invasion. His only real recreation was to go to church, but he went to parties when he had time. If he was in love with Rose Tramore this was distracting to him only in the same sense as his religion, and it was included in that department of his extremely sub-divided life. His religion indeed was of an encroaching. annexing sort. Seen from in front he looked diffident and blank, but he was capable of exposing himself in a way (to speak only of the paths of peace) wholly inconsistent with shyness. He had a passion for instance for open-air speaking, but was not thought on the whole to excel in it unless he could help himself out with a hymn. In conversation he kept his eyes on you with a kind of colourless candour, as if he had not understood what you were saying and, in a fashion that made many people turn red, waited before answering. This was only because he was considering their remarks in more relations than they had intended. He had in his face no expression whatever save the one just mentioned, and was, in his profession, already very distinguished.

He had seen Rose Tramore for the first time on a Sunday of the previous March, at a house in the country at which she was staying with her father, and five weeks later he had made her, by letter, an offer of marriage. She showed her father the letter of course, and he told her that it would give him great pleasure that she should send Captain Jay about his business. "My dear child," he said, "we must really have some one who will be better fun than that." Rose had declined the honour, very considerately and kindly, but not simply because her father wished it. She didn't herself wish to detach this flower from the stem, though when the young man wrote again, to express the hope that he MIGHT hope - so long was he willing to wait - and ask if he might not still sometimes see her, she answered even more indulgently than at first. She had shown her father her former letter, but she didn't show him this one; she only told him what it contained, submitting to him also that of her correspondent. Captain Jay moreover wrote to Mr. Tramore, who replied sociably, but so vaguely that he almost neglected the subject under discussion - a communication that made poor Bertram ponder long. He could never get to the bottom of the superficial, and all the proprieties and conventions of life were profound to him. Fortunately for him old Mrs. Tramore liked him, he was satisfactory to her long-sightedness; so that a relation was established under cover of which he still occasionally presented himself in Hill Street - presented himself nominally to the mistress of the house. He had had scruples about the veracity of his visits, but he had disposed of them; he had scruples about so many things that he had had to invent a general way, to dig a central drain. Julia Tramore happened to meet him when she came up to town, and she took a view of him more benevolent than her usual estimate of people encouraged by her mother. The fear of agreeing with that lady was a motive, but there was a stronger one, in this particular case, in the fear of agreeing with her niece, who had rejected him. His situation might be held to have improved when Mr. Tramore was taken so gravely ill that with regard to his recovery those about him left their eyes to speak for their lips; and in the light of the poor gentleman's recent death it was doubtless better than it had ever been.

He was only a quarter of an hour with the girl, but this gave him time to take the measure of it. After he had spoken to her about her bereavement, very much as an especially mild missionary might have spoken to a beautiful Polynesian, he let her know that he had learned from her companions the very strong step she was about to take. This led to their spending together ten minutes which, to her mind, threw more light on his character than anything that had ever passed between them. She had always felt with him as if she were standing on an edge, looking down into something decidedly deep. To-day the impression of the perpendicular shaft was there, but it was rather an abyss of confusion and disorder than the large bright space in which she had figured everything as ranged and pigeon-holed, presenting the appearance of the labelled shelves and drawers at a chemist's. He discussed without an invitation to discuss, he appealed without a right to appeal. He was nothing but a suitor tolerated after dismissal, but he took strangely for granted a participation in her affairs. He assumed all sorts of things that made her draw back. He implied that there was everything now to assist them in arriving at an agreement, since she had never informed him that he was positively objectionable; but that this symmetry would be spoiled if she should not be willing to take a little longer to think of certain consequences. She was greatly disconcerted when she saw what consequences he meant and at his reminding her of them. What on earth was the use of a lover if he was to speak only like one's grandmother and one's aunt? He struck her as much in love with her and as particularly careful at the same time as to what he might say. He never mentioned her mother; he only alluded, indirectly but earnestly, to the "step." He disapproved of it altogether, took an unexpectedly prudent, politic view of it. He evidently also believed that she would be dragged down; in other words that she would not be asked out. It was his idea that her mother would contaminate her, so that he should find himself interested in a young erson discredited and virtually unmarriageable. All this was more obvious to him than the consideration that a daughter should be merciful. Where was his religion if he understood mercy so little, and where were his talent and his courage if he were so miserably afraid of trumpery social penalties? Rose's heart sank when she reflected that a man supposed to be first-rate hadn't guessed that rather than not do what she could for her mother she would give up all the Engineers in the world. She became aware that she probably would have been moved to place her hand in his on the spot if he had come to her saying "Your idea is the right one; put it through at every cost." She couldn't discuss this with him, though he impressed her as having too much at stake for her to

Henry James

treat him with mere disdain. She sickened at the revelation that a gentleman could see so much in mere vulgarities of opinion, and though she uttered as few words as possible, conversing only in sad smiles and headshakes and in intercepted movements toward the door, she happened, in some unguarded lapse from her reticence, to use the expression that she was disappointed in him. He caught at it and, seeming to drop his field-glass, pressed upon her with nearer, tenderer eyes.

"Can I be so happy as to believe, then, that you had thought of me with some confidence, with some faith?"

"If you didn't suppose so, what is the sense of this visit?" Rose asked.

"One can be faithful without reciprocity," said the young man. "I regard you in a light which makes me want to protect you even if I have nothing to gain by it."

"Yet you speak as if you thought you might keep me for yourself."

"For YOURSELF. I don't want you to suffer."

"Nor to suffer yourself by my doing so," said Rose, looking down.

"Ah, if you would only marry me next month!" he broke out inconsequently.

"And give up going to mamma?" Rose waited to see if he would say "What need that matter? Can't your mother come to us?" But he said nothing of the sort; he only answered -

"She surely would be sorry to interfere with the exercise of any other affection which I might have the bliss of believing that you are now free, in however small a degree, to entertain."

Rose knew that her mother wouldn't be sorry at all; but she contented herself with rejoining, her hand on the door: "Good-bye. I sha'n't suffer. I'm not afraid."

"You don't know how terrible, how cruel, the world can be."

"Yes, I do know. I know everything!"

The declaration sprang from her lips in a tone which made him look at her as he had never looked before, as if he saw something new in her face, as if he had never yet known her. He hadn't displeased her so much but that she would like to give him that impression, and since she felt that she was doing so she lingered an instant for the purpose. It enabled her to see, further, that he turned red; then to become aware that a carriage had stopped at the door. Captain Jay's eyes, from where he stood, fell upon this arrival, and the nature of their glance made Rose step forward to look. Her mother sat there, brilliant, conspicuous, in the eternal victoria, and the footman was already sounding the knocker. It had been no part of the arrangement that she should come to fetch her; it had been out of the question - a stroke in such bad taste as would have put Rose in the wrong. The girl had never dreamed of it, but somehow, suddenly, perversely, she was glad of it now; she even hoped that her grandmother and her

Henry James

aunt were looking out upstairs.

"My mother has come for me. Good-bye," she repeated; but this time her visitor had got between her and the door.

"Listen to me before you go. I will give you a life's devotion," the young man pleaded. He really barred the way.

She wondered whether her grandmother had told him that if her flight were not prevented she would forfeit money. Then, vividly, it came over her that this would be what he was occupied with. "I shall never think of you - let me go!" she cried, with passion.

Captain Jay opened the door, but Rose didn't see his face, and in a moment she was out of the house. Aunt Julia, who was sure to have been hovering, had taken flight before the profanity of the knock.

"Heavens, dear, where did you get your mourning?" the lady in the victoria asked of her daughter as they drove away.

CHAPTER II.

Lady Maresfield had given her boy a push in his plump back and had said to him, "Go and speak to her now; it's your chance." She had for a long time wanted this scion to make himself audible to Rose Tramore, but the opportunity was not easy to come by. The case was complicated. Lady Maresfield had four daughters, of whom only one was married. It so happened moreover that this one, Mrs. Vaughan-Vesey, the only person in the world her mother was afraid of, was the most to be reckoned with. The Honourable Guy was in appearance all his mother's child, though he was really a simpler soul. He was large and pink; large, that is, as to everything but the eyes, which were diminishing points, and pink as to everything but the hair, which was comparable, faintly, to the hue of the richer rose. He had also, it must be conceded, very small neat teeth, which made his smile look like a young lady's. He had no wish to resemble any such person, but he was perpetually smiling, and he smiled more than ever as he approached Rose Tramore, who, looking altogether, to his mind, as a pretty girl should, and wearing a soft white opera-cloak over a softer black dress, leaned alone against the wall of the vestibule at Covent Garden while, a few paces off, an old gentleman engaged her mother in conversation. Madame Patti had been singing, and they were all waiting for their carriages. To their ears at present came a vociferation of names and a rattle of wheels. The air, through banging doors, entered in damp, warm gusts, heavy with the stale, slightly sweet taste of the London season when the London season is overripe and spoiling.

Guy Mangler had only three minutes to reestablish an interrupted acquaintance with our young lady. He reminded her that he had danced with her the year before, and he mentioned that he knew her brother. His mother had lately been to see old Mrs. Tramore, but this he did not mention, not being aware of it. That visit had produced, on Lady Maresfield's part, a private crisis, engendered ideas. One of them was that the grandmother in Hill Street had really forgiven the wilful girl much more than she admitted. Another was that there would still be some money for Rose when the others should come into theirs. Still another was that the others would come into theirs at no distant date; the old lady was so visibly going to pieces. There were several more besides, as for instance that Rose had already fifteen hundred a year from her father. The figure had been betrayed in Hill Street; it was part of the proof of Mrs. Tramore's decrepitude. Then there was an equal amount that her mother had to dispose of and on which the girl could absolutely count, though of course it might involve much waiting, as the mother, a person of gross insensibility, evidently wouldn't die of cold-shouldering. Equally definite, to do it justice, was the conception that Rose was in truth remarkably good looking, and that what she had undertaken to do showed, and would show even should it fail, cleverness of the right sort. Cleverness of the right sort was exactly the quality that Lady Maresfield prefigured as indispensable in a young lady to whom she should marry her second son, over whose own deficiencies she flung the veil of a maternal theory that HIS cleverness was of a sort that was wrong. Those who knew him less well were content to wish that he might not conceal it for such a scruple. This enumeration of his mother's views does not exhaust the list, and it was in obedience to one too profound to be uttered even by the historian that, after a very brief delay, she decided to move across the crowded lobby. Her daughter Bessie was the only one with her; Maggie was dining with the Vaughan-Veseys, and Fanny was not of an age. Mrs. Tramore the younger showed only an admirable back - her face was to her old gentleman - and Bessie had drifted to some other people; so that it was comparatively easy for Lady Maresfield to say to Rose, in a moment: "My dear child, are you never coming to see us?"

"We shall be delighted to come if you'll ask us," Rose smiled.

Lady Maresfield had been prepared for the plural number, and she was a woman whom it took many plurals to disconcert. "I'm sure Guy is longing for another dance with you," she rejoined, with the most unblinking irrelevance.

"I'm afraid we're not dancing again quite yet," said Rose, glancing at her mother's exposed shoulders, but speaking as if they were muffled in crape.

Lady Maresfield leaned her head on one side and seemed almost wistful. "Not even at my sister's ball? She's to have something next week. She'll write to you."

Rose Tramore, on the spot, looking bright but vague,

turned three or four things over in her mind. She remembered that the sister of her interlocutress was the proverbially rich Mrs. Bray, a bankeress or a breweress or a builderess, who had so big a house that she couldn't fill it unless she opened her doors, or her mouth, very wide. Rose had learnt more about London society during these lonely months with her mother than she had ever picked up in Hill Street. The younger Mrs. Tramore was a mine of commerages, and she had no need to go out to bring home the latest intelligence. At any rate Mrs. Bray might serve as the end of a wedge. "Oh, I dare say we might think of that," Rose said. "It would be very kind of your sister."

"Guy'll think of it, won't you, Guy?" asked Lady Maresfield.

"Rather!" Guy responded, with an intonation as fine as if he had learnt it at a music hall; while at the same moment the name of his mother's carriage was bawled through the place. Mrs. Tramore had parted with her old gentleman; she turned again to her daughter. Nothing occurred but what always occurred, which was exactly this absence of everything - a universal lapse. She didn't exist, even for a second, to any recognising eye. The people who looked at her - of course there were plenty of those - were only the people who didn't exist for hers. Lady Maresfield surged away on her son's arm.

It was this noble matron herself who wrote, the next day, inclosing a card of invitation from Mrs. Bray and expressing the hope that Rose would come and dine and let her ladyship take her. She should have only one of her own girls; Gwendolen Vesey was to take the other. Rose handed both the note and the card in silence to her mother; the latter exhibited only the name of Miss Tramore. "You had much better go, dear," her mother said; in answer to which Miss Tramore slowly tore up the documents, looking with clear, meditative eyes out of the window. Her mother always said "You had better go" - there had been other incidents - and Rose had never even once taken account of the observation. She would make no first advances, only plenty of second ones, and, condoning no discrimination, would treat no omission as venial. She would keep all concessions till afterwards; then she would make them one by one. Fighting society was quite as hard as her grandmother had said it would be; but there was a tension in it which made the dreariness vibrate - the dreariness of such a winter as she had just passed. Her companion had cried at the end of it, and she had cried all through; only her tears had been private, while her mother's had fallen once for all, at luncheon on the bleak Easter Monday - produced by the way a silent survey of the deadly square brought home to her that every creature but themselves was out of town and having tremendous fun. Rose felt that it was useless to attempt to explain simply by her mourning this severity of solitude; for if people didn't go to parties (at least a few didn't) for six months after their father died, this was the very time other people took for coming to see them. It was not too much to say that during this first winter of Rose's period with her mother she had no communication whatever with the world. It had the effect of making her take to reading the new American books: she wanted to see how girls got on by themselves. She had never read so much before, and there was a legitimate indifference in it when topics failed with her mother. They often failed after the first days, and then, while she bent over instructive volumes, this lady, dressed as if for an

Henry James

impending function, sat on the sofa and watched her. Rose was not embarrassed by such an appearance, for she could reflect that, a little before, her companion had not ever a girl who had taken refuge in queer researches to look at. She was moreover used to her mother's attitude by this time. She had her own description of it: it was the attitude of waiting for the carriage. If they didn't go out it was not that Mrs. Tramore was not ready in time, and Rose had even an alarmed prevision of their some day always arriving first. Mrs. Tramore's conversation at such moments was abrupt, inconsequent and personal. She sat on the edge of sofas and chairs and glanced occasionally at the fit of her gloves (she was perpetually gloved, and the fit was a thing it was melancholy to see wasted), as people do who are expecting guests to dinner. Rose used almost to fancy herself at times a perfunctory husband on the other side of the fire.

What she was not yet used to - there was still a charm in it - was her mother's extraordinary tact. During the years they lived together they never had a discussion; a circumstance all the more remarkable since if the girl had a reason for sparing her companion (that of being sorry for her) Mrs. Tramore had none for sparing her child. She only showed in doing so a happy instinct - the happiest thing about her. She took in perfection a course which represented everything and covered everything; she utterly abjured all authority. She testified to her abjuration in hourly ingenious, touching ways. In this manner nothing had to be talked over, which was a mercy all round. The tears on Easter Monday were merely a nervous gust, to help show she was not a Christmas doll from the Burlington Arcade; and there was no lifting up of the repentant Magdalen, no uttered remorse for the former abandonment of children. Of the way she could treat her children her demeanour to this one was an example; it was an uninterrupted appeal to her eldest daughter for direction. She took the law from Rose in every circumstance, and if you had noticed these ladies without knowing their history you would have wondered what tie was fine enough to make maturity so respectful to youth. No mother was ever so filial as Mrs. Tramore, and there had never been such a difference of position between sisters. Not that the elder one fawned, which would have been fearful; she only renounced - whatever she had to renounce. If the amount was not much she at any rate made no scene over it. Her hand was so light that Rose said of her secretly, in vague glances at the past, "No wonder people liked her!" She never characterised the old element of interference with her mother's respectability more definitely than as "people." They were people, it was true, for whom gentleness must have been everything and who didn't demand a variety of interests. The desire to "go out" was the one passion that even a closer acquaintance with her parent revealed to Rose Tramore. She marvelled at its strength, in the light of the poor lady's history: there was comedy enough in this unquenchable flame on the part of a woman who had known such misery. She had drunk deep of every dishonour, but the bitter cup had left her with a taste for lighted candles, for squeezing up staircases and hooking herself to the human elbow. Rose had a vision of the future years in which this taste would grow with restored exercise - of her mother, in a long-tailed dress, jogging on and on and on, jogging further and further from her sins, through a century of the "Morning Post" and down the fashionable avenue of time. She herself would then be very old - she herself would be dead. Mrs. Tramore would cover a span of life for which such an allowance of sin was small. The girl could laugh indeed now at that theory of her being dragged down. If one thing were more present to her than another it was the very desolation of their propriety. As she glanced at her companion, it sometimes seemed to her that if she had been a bad woman she would have been worse than that. There were compensations for being "cut" which Mrs. Tramore too much neglected.

The lonely old lady in Hill Street - Rose thought of her that way now - was the one person to whom she was ready to say that she would come to her on any terms. She wrote this to her three times over, and she knocked still oftener at her door. But the old lady answered no letters; if Rose had remained in Hill Street it would have been her own function to answer them; and at the door, the butler, whom the girl had known for ten years, considered her, when he told her his mistress was not at home, quite as he might have considered a young person who had come about a place and of whose eligibility he took a negative view. That was Rose's one pang, that she probably appeared rather heartless. Her aunt Julia had gone to Florence with Edith for the winter, on purpose to make her appear more so; for Miss Tramore was still the person most scandalised by her secession. Edith and she, doubtless, often talked over in Florence the destitution of the aged victim in Hill Street. Eric never came to see his sister, because, being full both of family and of personal feeling, he thought she really ought to have stayed with his grandmother. If she had had such an appurtenance all to herself she might have done what she liked with it; but he couldn't forgive such a want of consideration for anything of his. There were moments when Rose would have been ready to take her hand from the plough and insist upon reintegration, if only the fierce voice of the old house had allowed people to look her up. But she read, ever so clearly, that her grandmother had made this a question of loyalty to seventy years of virtue. Mrs. Tramore's forlornness didn't prevent her drawing-room from being a very public place, in which Rose could hear certain words reverberate: "Leave her alone; it's the only way to see how long she'll hold out." The old woman's visitors were people who didn't wish to quarrel, and the girl was conscious that if they had not let her alone - that is if they had come to her from her grandmother - she might perhaps not have held out. She had no friends quite of her own; she had not been brought up to have them, and it would not have been easy in a house which two such persons as her father and his mother divided between them. Her father disapproved of crude intimacies, and all the intimacies of youth were crude. He had married at five-and-twenty and could testify to such a truth. Rose felt that she shared even Captain Jay with her grandmother; she had seen what HE was worth. Moreover, she had spoken to him at that last moment in Hill Street in a way which, taken with her former refusal, made it impossible that he should come near her again. She hoped he went to see his protectress: he could be a kind of substitute and administer comfort.

It so happened, however, that the day after she threw Lady Maresfield's invitation into the wastepaper basket she received a visit from a certain Mrs. Donovan, whom she had occasionally seen in Hill Street. She vaguely knew this lady for a busybody, but she was in a situation which even busybodies might alleviate. Mrs. Donovan was poor, but honest - so scrupulously honest that she was perpetually returning visits she had never received. She was always clad in weather-beaten sealskin, and had an odd air of being prepared for the worst, which was borne out by her denying that she was Irish. She was of the English Donovans.

"Dear child, won't you go out with me?" she asked.

Rose looked at her a moment and then rang the bell. She spoke of something else, without answering the question, and when the servant came she said: "Please tell Mrs. Tramore that Mrs. Donovan has come to see her."

"Oh, that'll be delightful; only you mustn't tell your grandmother!" the visitor exclaimed.

"Tell her what?"

"That I come to see your mamma."

"You don't," said Rose.

"Sure I hoped you'd introduce me!" cried Mrs. Donovan, compromising herself in her embarrassment.

"It's not necessary; you knew her once."

"Indeed and I've known every one once," the visitor confessed.

Mrs. Tramore, when she came in, was charming and exactly right; she greeted Mrs. Donovan as if she had met her the week before last, giving her daughter such a new illustration of her tact that Rose again had the idea that it was no wonder "people" had liked her. The girl grudged Mrs. Donovan so fresh a morsel as a description of her mother at home, rejoicing that she would be inconvenienced by having to keep the story out of Hill Street. Her mother went away before Mrs. Donovan departed, and Rose was touched by guessing her reason - the thought that since even this circuitous personage had been moved to come, the two might, if left together, invent some remedy. Rose waited to see what Mrs. Donovan had in fact invented.

"You won't come out with me then?"

"Come out with you?"

"My daughters are married. You know I'm a lone woman. It would be an immense pleasure to me to have so charming a creature as yourself to present to the world."

"I go out with my mother," said Rose, after a moment.

"Yes, but sometimes when she's not inclined?"

"She goes everywhere she wants to go," Rose continued, uttering the biggest fib of her life and only regretting it should be wasted on Mrs. Donovan.

"Ah, but do you go everywhere YOU want?" the lady asked sociably.

"One goes even to places one hates. Every one does that."

"Oh, what I go through!" this social martyr cried. Then she laid a persuasive hand on the girl's arm. "Let me show you at a few places first, and then we'll see. I'll bring them all here."

"I don't think I understand you," replied Rose, though in Mrs. Donovan's words she perfectly saw her own theory of the case reflected. For a quarter of a minute she asked herself whether she might not, after all, do so much evil that good might come. Mrs. Donovan would take her out the next day, and be thankful enough to annex such an attraction as a pretty girl. Various consequences would ensue and the long delay would be shortened; her mother's drawing-room would resound with the clatter of teacups.

"Mrs. Bray's having some big thing next week; come with me there and I'll show you what I mane," Mrs. Donovan pleaded.

"I see what you mane," Rose answered, brushing away her temptation and getting up. "I'm much obliged to you."

"You know you're wrong, my dear," said her interlocutress, with angry little eyes.

"I'm not going to Mrs. Bray's."

"I'll get you a kyard; it'll only cost me a penny stamp."

"I've got one," said the girl, smiling.

"Do you mean a penny stamp?" Mrs. Donovan, especially at departure, always observed all the forms of amity. "You can't do it alone, my darling," she declared.

"Shall they call you a cab?" Rose asked.

"I'll pick one up. I choose my horse. You know you

require your start," her visitor went on.

"Excuse my mother," was Rose's only reply.

"Don't mention it. Come to me when you need me. You'll find me in the Red Book."

"It's awfully kind of you."

Mrs. Donovan lingered a moment on the threshold. "Who will you HAVE now, my child?" she appealed.

"I won't have any one!" Rose turned away, blushing for her. "She came on speculation," she said afterwards to Mrs. Tramore.

Her mother looked at her a moment in silence. "You can do it if you like, you know."

Rose made no direct answer to this observation; she remarked instead: "See what our quiet life allows us to escape."

"We don't escape it. She has been here an hour."

"Once in twenty years! We might meet her three times a day."

"Oh, I'd take her with the rest!" sighed Mrs. Tramore; while her daughter recognised that what her companion wanted to do was just what Mrs. Donovan was doing. Mrs. Donovan's life was her ideal.

On a Sunday, ten days later, Rose went to see one of her old governesses, of whom she had lost sight for some time and who had written to her that she was in

London, unoccupied and ill. This was just the sort of relation into which she could throw herself now with inordinate zeal; the idea of it, however, not preventing a foretaste of the queer expression in the excellent lady's face when she should mention with whom she was living. While she smiled at this picture she threw in another joke, asking herself if Miss Hack could be held in any degree to constitute the nucleus of a circle. She would come to see her, in any event - come the more the further she was dragged down. Sunday was always a difficult day with the two ladies - the afternoons made it so apparent that they were not frequented. Her mother, it is true, was comprised in the habits of two or three old gentlemen - she had for a long time avoided male friends of less than seventy - who disliked each other enough to make the room, when they were there at once, crack with pressure. Rose sat for a long time with Miss Hack, doing conscientious justice to the conception that there could be troubles in the world worse than her own; and when she came back her mother was alone, but with a story to tell of a long visit from Mr. Guy Mangler, who had waited and waited for her return. "He's in love with you; he's coming again on Tuesday," Mrs. Tramore announced.

"Did he say so?"

"That he's coming back on Tuesday?"

"No, that he's in love with me."

"He didn't need, when he stayed two hours."

"With you? It's you he's in love with, mamma!"

"That will do as well," laughed Mrs. Tramore. "For all the use we shall make of him!" she added in a moment.

"We shall make great use of him. His mother sent him."

"Oh, she'll never come!"

"Then HE sha'n't," said Rose. Yet he was admitted on the Tuesday, and after she had given him his tea Mrs. Tramore left the young people alone. Rose wished she hadn't - she herself had another view. At any rate she disliked her mother's view, which she had easily guessed. Mr. Mangler did nothing but say how charming he thought his hostess of the Sunday, and what a tremendously jolly visit he had had. He didn't remark in so many words "I had no idea your mother was such a good sort"; but this was the spirit of his simple discourse. Rose liked it at first - a little of it gratified her; then she thought there was too much of it for good taste. She had to reflect that one does what one can and that Mr. Mangler probably thought he was delicate. He wished to convey that he desired to make up to her for the injustice of society. Why shouldn't her mother receive gracefully, she asked (not audibly) and who had ever said she didn't? Mr. Mangler had a great deal to say about the disappointment of his own parent over Miss Tramore's not having come to dine with them the night of his aunt's ball.

"Lady Maresfield knows why I didn't come," Rose answered at last.

"Ah, now, but *I* don't, you know; can't you tell ME?" asked the young man.

"It doesn't matter, if your mother's clear about it."

"Oh, but why make such an awful mystery of it, when I'm dying to know?"

He talked about this, he chaffed her about it for the rest of his visit: he had at last found a topic after his own heart. If her mother considered that he might be the emblem of their redemption he was an engine of the most primitive construction. He stayed and stayed; he struck Rose as on the point of bringing out something for which he had not quite, as he would have said, the cheek. Sometimes she thought he was going to begin: "By the way, my mother told me to propose to you." At other moments he seemed charged with the admission: "I say, of course I really know what you're trying to do for her," nodding at the door: "therefore hadn't we better speak of it frankly, so that I can help you with my mother, and more particularly with my sister Gwendolen, who's the difficult one? The fact is, you see, they won't do anything for nothing. If you'll accept me they'll call, but they won't call without something 'down.'" Mr. Mangler departed without their speaking frankly, and Rose Tramore had a hot hour during which she almost entertained, vindictively, the project of "accepting" the limpid youth until after she should have got her mother into circulation. The cream of the vision was that she might break with him later. She could read that this was what her mother would have liked, but the next time he came the door was closed to him, and the next and the next.

In August there was nothing to do but to go abroad, with the sense on Rose's part that the battle was still all to fight; for a round of country visits was not in prospect, and English watering-places constituted one of the few subjects on which the girl had heard her mother express herself with disgust. Continental autumns had been indeed for years, one of the various forms of Mrs. Tramore's atonement, but Rose could only infer that such fruit as they had borne was bitter. The stony stare of Belgravia could be practised at Homburg; and somehow it was inveterately only gentlemen who sat next to her at the table d'hote at Cadenabbia. Gentlemen hd never been of any use to Mrs. Tramore for getting back into society; they had only helped her effectually to get out of it. She once dropped, to her daughter, in a moralising mood, the remark that it was astonishing how many of them one could know without its doing one any good. Fifty of them - even very clever ones - represented a value inferior to that of one stupid woman. Rose wondered at the offhand way in which her mother could talk of fifty clever men; it seemed to her that the whole world couldn't contain such a number. She had a sombre sense that mankind must be dull and mean. These cogitations took place in a cold hotel, in an eternal Swiss rain, and they had a flat echo in the transalpine valleys, as the lonely ladies went vaguely down to the Italian lakes and cities. Rose guided their course, at moments, with a kind of aimless ferocity; she moved abruptly, feeling vulgar and hating their life, though destitute of any definite vision of another life that would have been open to her. She had set herself a task and she clung to it; but she appeared to herself despicably idle. She had succeeded in not going to Homburg waters, where London was trying to wash away some of its stains; that would be too staring an advertisement of their situation. The main difference in situations to her now was the difference of being more or less pitied, at the best an intolerable danger; so that the places she preferred were the unsuspicious ones.

Henry James

She wanted to triumph with contempt, not with submission.

One morning in September, coming with her mother out of the marble church at Milan, she perceived that a gentleman who had just passed her on his way into the cathedral and whose face she had not noticed, had quickly raised his hat, with a suppressed ejaculation. She involuntarily glanced back; the gentleman had paused, again uncovering, and Captain Jay stood saluting her in the Italian sunshine. "Oh, good-morning!" she said, and walked on, pursuing her course; her mother was a little in front. She overtook her in a moment, with an unreasonable sense, like a gust of cold air, that men were worse than ever, for Captain Jay had apparently moved into the church. Her mother turned as they met, and suddenly, as she looked back, an expression of peculiar sweetness came into this lady's eyes. It made Rose's take the same direction and rest a second time on Captain Jay, who was planted just where he had stood a minute before. He immediately came forward, asking Rose with great gravity if he might speak to her a moment, while Mrs. Tramore went her way again. He had the expression of a man who wished to say something very important; yet his next words were simple enough and consisted of the remark that he had not seen her for a year.

"Is it really so much as that?" asked Rose.

"Very nearly. I would have looked you up, but in the first place I have been very little in London, and in the second I believed it wouldn't have done any good."

"You should have put that first," said the girl. "It wouldn't have done any good."

He was silent over this a moment, in his customary deciphering way; but the view he took of it did not prevent him from inquiring, as she slowly followed her mother, if he mightn't walk with her now. She answered with a laugh that it wouldn't do any good but that he might do as he liked. He replied without the slightest manifestation of levity that it would do more good than if he didn't, and they strolled together, with Mrs. Tramore well before them, across the big, amusing piazza, where the front of the cathedral makes a sort of builded light. He asked a question or two and he explained his own presence: having a month's holiday, the first clear time for several years, he had just popped over the Alps. He inquired if Rose had recent news of the old lady in Hill Street, and it was the only tortuous thing she had ever heard him say.

"I have had no communication of any kind from her since I parted with you under her roof. Hasn't she mentioned that?" said Rose.

"I haven't seen her."

"I thought you were such great friends."

Bertram Jay hesitated a moment. "Well, not so much now."

"What has she done to you?" Rose demanded.

He fidgeted a little, as if he were thinking of something that made him unconscious of her question; then, with mild violence, he brought out the inquiry: "Miss Tramore, are you happy?"

She was startled by the words, for she on her side had

been reflecting - reflecting that he had broken with her grandmother and that this pointed to a reason. It suggested at least that he wouldn't now be so much like a mouthpiece for that cold ancestral tone. She turned off his question - said it never was a fair one, as you gave yourself away however you answered it. When he repeated "You give yourself away?" as if he didn't understand, she remembered that he had not read the funny American books. This brought them to a silence, for she had enlightened him only by another laugh, and he was evidently preparing another question, which he wished carefully to disconnect from the former. Presently, just as they were coming near Mrs. Tramore, it arrived in the words "Is this lady your mother?" On Rose's assenting, with the addition that she was travelling with her, he said: "Will you be so kind as to introduce me to her?" They were so close to Mrs. Tramore that she probably heard, but she floated away with a single stroke of her paddle and an inattentive poise of her head. It was a striking exhibition of the famous tact, for Rose delayed to answer, which was exactly what might have made her mother wish to turn; and indeed when at last the girl spoke she only said to her companion: "Why do you ask me that?"

"Because I desire the pleasure of making her acquaintance."

Rose had stopped, and in the middle of the square they stood looking at each other. "Do you remember what you said to me the last time I saw you?"

"Oh, don't speak of that!"

"It's better to speak of it now than to speak of it later."

Bertram Jay looked round him, as if to see whether any one would hear; but the bright foreignness gave him a sense of safety, and he unexpectedly exclaimed: "Miss Tramore, I love you more than ever!"

"Then you ought to have come to see us," declared the girl, quickly walking on.

"You treated me the last time as if I were positively offensive to you."

"So I did, but you know my reason."

"Because I protested against the course you were taking? I did, I did!" the young man rang out, as if he still, a little, stuck to that.

His tone made Rose say gaily: "Perhaps you do so yet?"

"I can't tell till I've seen more of your circumstances," he replied with eminent honesty.

The girl stared; her light laugh filled the air. "And it's in order to see more of them and judge that you wish to make my mother's acquaintance?"

He coloured at this and he evaded; then he broke out with a confused "Miss Tramore, let me stay with you a little!" which made her stop again.

"Your company will do us great honour, but there must be a rigid condition attached to our acceptance of it."

"Kindly mention it," said Captain Jay, staring at the facade of the cathedral.

"You don't take us on trial."

"On trial?"

"You don't make an observation to me - not a single one, ever, ever! - on the matter that, in Hill Street, we had our last words about."

Captain Jay appeared to be counting the thousand pinnacles of the church. "I think you really must be right," he remarked at last.

"There you are!" cried Rose Tramore, and walked rapidly away.

He caught up with her, he laid his hand upon her arm to stay her. "If you're going to Venice, let me go to Venice with you!"

"You don't even understand my condition."

"I'm sure you're right, then: you must be right about everything."

"That's not in the least true, and I don't care a fig whether you're sure or not. Please let me go."

He had barred her way, he kept her longer. "I'll go and speak to your mother myself!"

Even in the midst of another emotion she was amused at the air of audacity accompanying this declaration. Poor Captain Jay might have been on the point of marching up to a battery. She looked at him a moment; then she said: "You'll be disappointed!"

"Disappointed?"

"She's much more proper than grandmamma, because she's much more amiable."

"Dear Miss Tramore - dear Miss Tramore!" the young man murmured helplessly.

"You'll see for yourself. Only there's another condition," Rose went on.

"Another?" he cried, with discouragement and alarm.

"You must understand thoroughly, before you throw in your lot with us even for a few days, what our position really is."

"Is it very bad?" asked Bertram Jay artlessly.

"No one has anything to do with us, no one speaks to us, no one looks at us."

"Really?" stared the young man.

"We've no social existence, we're utterly despised."

"Oh, Miss Tramore!" Captain Jay interposed. He added quickly, vaguely, and with a want of presence of mind of which he as quickly felt ashamed: "Do none of your family - ?" The question collapsed; the brilliant girl was looking at him.

"We're extraordinarily happy," she threw out.

"Now that's all I wanted to know!" he exclaimed, with a kind of exaggerated cheery reproach, walking on with her briskly to overtake her mother.

He was not dining at their inn, but he insisted on coming that evening to their table d'hote. He sat next Mrs. Tramore, and in the evening he accompanied them gallantly to the opera, at a third-rate theatre where they were almost the only ladies in the boxes. The next day they went together by rail to the Charterhouse of Pavia, and while he strolled with the girl, as they waited for the homeward train, he said to her candidly: "Your mother's remarkably pretty." She remembered the words and the feeling they gave her: they were the first note of new era. The feeling was somewhat that of an anxious, gratified matron who has "presented" her child and is thinking of the matrimonial market. Men might be of no use, as Mrs. Tramore said, yet it was from this moment Rose dated the rosy dawn of her confidence that her protegee would go off; and when later, in crowded assemblies, the phrase, or something like it behind a hat or a fan, fell repeatedly on her anxious ear, "Your mother IS in beauty!" or 'I've never seen her look better!" she had a faint vision of the yellow sunshine and the afternoon shadows on the dusty Italian platform.

Mrs. Tramore's behaviour at this period was a revelation of her native understanding of delicate situations. She needed no account of this one from her daughter - it was one of the things for which she had a scent; and there was a kind of loyalty to the rules of a game in the silent sweetness with which she smoothed the path of Bertram Jay. It was clear that she was in her element in fostering the exercise of the affections, and if she ever spoke without thinking twice it is probable that she would have exclaimed, with some gaiety, "Oh, I know all about LOVE!" Rose could see that she thought their companion would be a help, in spite of his being no dispenser of patronage. The key to the gates of fashion had not been placed in his hand, and no one had ever heard of the ladies of his family, who lived in some vague hollow of the Yorkshire moors; but none the less he might administer a muscular push. Yes indeed, men in general were broken reeds, but Captain Jay was peculiarly representative. Respectability was the woman's maximum, as honour was the man's, but this distinguished young soldier inspired more than one kind of confidence. Rose had a great deal of attention for the use to which his respectability was put; and there mingled with this attention some amusement and much compassion. She saw that after a couple of days he decidedly liked her mother, and that he was yet not in the least aware of it. He took for granted that he believed in her but little; notwithstanding which he would have trusted her with anything except Rose herself. His trusting her with Rose would come very soon. He never spoke to her daughter about her qualities of character, but two or three of them (and indeed these were all the poor lady had, and they made the best show) were what he had in mind in praising her appearance. When he remarked: "What attention Mrs. Tramore seems to attract everywhere!" he meant: "What a beautifully simple nature it is!" and when he said: "There's something extraordinarily harmonious in the colours she wears," it signified: "Upon my word, I never saw such a sweet temper in my life!" She lost one of her boxes at Verona, and made the prettiest joke of it to Captain Jay. When Rose saw this she said to herself, "Next season we shall have only to choose." Rose knew what was in the box.

By the time they reached Venice (they had stopped at

half a dozen little old romantic cities in the most frolicsome aesthetic way) she liked their companion better than she had ever liked him before. She did him the justice to recognise that if he was not quite honest with himself he was at least wholly honest with HER. She reckoned up everything he had been since he joined them, and put upon it all an interpretation so favourable to his devotion that, catching herself in the act of glossing over one or two episodes that had not struck her at the time as disinterested she exclaimed, beneath her breath, "Look out - you're falling in love!" But if he liked correctness wasn't he quite right? Could any one possibly like it more than SHE did? And if he had protested against her throwing in her lot with her mother, this was not because of the benefit conferred but because of the injury received. He exaggerated that injury, but this was the privilege of a lover perfectly willing to be selfish on behalf of his mistress. He might have wanted her grandmother's money for her, but if he had given her up on first discovering that she was throwing away her chance of it (oh, this was HER doing too!) he had given up her grandmother as much: not keeping well with the old woman, as some men would have done; not waiting to see how the perverse experiment would turn out and appeasing her, if it should promise tolerably, with a view to future operations. He had had a simple-minded, evangelical, lurid view of what the girl he loved would find herself in for. She could see this now - she could see it from his present bewilderment and mystification, and she liked him and pitied him, with the kindest smile, for the original naivete as well as for the actual meekness. No wonder he hadn't known what she was in for, since he now didn't even know what he was in for himself. Were there not moments when he thought his companions almost unnaturally good, almost suspiciously safe? He had lost all power to verify that sketch of their isolation and declassement to which she had treated him on the great square at Milan. The last thing he noticed was that they were neglected, and he had never, for himself, had such an impression of society.

It could scarcely be enhanced even by the apparition of a large, fair, hot, red-haired young man, carrying a lady's fan in his hand, who suddenly stood before their little party as, on the third evening after their arrival in Venice, it partook of ices at one of the tables before the celebrated Cafe Florian. The lamplit Venetian dusk appeared to have revealed them to this gentleman as he sat with other friends at a neighbouring table, and he had sprung up, with unsophisticated glee, to shake hands with Mrs. Tramore and her daughter. Rose recalled him to her mother, who looked at first as though she didn't remember him but presently bestowed a sufficiently gracious smile on Mr. Guy Mangler. He gave with youthful candour the history of his movements and indicated the whereabouts of his family: he was with his mother and sisters; they had met the Bob Veseys, who had taken Lord Whiteroy's yacht and were going to Constantinople. His mother and the girls, poor things, were at the Grand Hotel, but he was on the yacht with the Veseys, where they had Lord Whiteroy's cook. Wasn't the food in Venice filthy, and wouldn't they come and look at the yacht? She wasn't very fast, but she was awfully jolly. His mother might have come if she would, but she wouldn't at first, and now, when she wanted to, there were other people, who naturally wouldn't turn out for her. Mr. Mangler sat down; he alluded with artless resentment to the way, in July, the door of his friends had been closed to him. He was going to

Constantinople, but he didn't care - if THEY were going anywhere; meanwhile his mother hoped awfully they would look her up.

Lady Maresfield, if she had given her son any such message, which Rose disbelieved, entertained her hope in a manner compatible with her sitting for half an hour, surrounded by her little retinue, without glancing in the direction of Mrs. Tramore. The girl, however, was aware that this was not a good enough instance of their humiliation; inasmuch as it was rather she who, on the occasion of their last contact, had held off from Lady Maresfield. She was a little ashamed now of not having answered the note in which this affable personage ignored her mother. She couldn't help perceiving indeed a dim movement on the part of some of the other members of the group; she made out an attitude of observation in the high-plumed head of Mrs. Vaughan-Vesey. Mrs. Vesey, perhaps, might have been looking at Captain Jay, for as this gentleman walked back to the hotel with our young lady (they were at the "Britannia," and young Mangler, who clung to them, went in front with Mrs. Tramore) he revealed to Rose that he had some acquaintance with Lady Maresfield's eldest daughter, though he didn't know and didn't particularly want to know, her ladyship. He expressed himself with more acerbity than she had ever heard him use (Christian charity so generally governed his speech) about the young donkey who had been prattling to them. They separated at the door of the hotel. Mrs. Tramore had got rid of Mr. Mangler, and Bertram Jay was in other quarters.

"If you know Mrs. Vesey, why didn't you go and speak to her? I'm sure she saw you," Rose said.

Captain Jay replied even more circumspectly than usual. "Because I didn't want to leave you."

"Well, you can go now; you're free," Rose rejoined.

"Thank you. I shall never go again."

"That won't be civil," said Rose.

"I don't care to be civil. I don't like her."

"Why don't you like her?"

"You ask too many questions."

"I know I do," the girl acknowledged.

Captain Jay had already shaken hands with her, but at this he put out his hand again. "She's too worldly," he murmured, while he held Rose Tramore's a moment.

"Ah, you dear!" Rose exclaimed almost audibly as, with her mother, she turned away.

The next morning, upon the Grand Canal, the gondola of our three friends encountered a stately barge which, though it contained several persons, seemed pervaded mainly by one majestic presence. During the instant the gondolas were passing each other it was impossible either for Rose Tramore or for her companions not to become conscious that this distinguished identity had markedly inclined itself - a circumstance commemorated the next moment, almost within earshot of the other boat, by the most spontaneous cry that had issued for many a day from the lips of Mrs. Tramore. "Fancy, my dear, Lady Maresfield has bowed to us!"

"We ought to have returned it," Rose answered; but she looked at Bertram Jay, who was opposite to her. He blushed, and she blushed, and during this moment was born a deeper understanding than had yet existed between these associated spirits. It had something to do with their going together that afternoon, without her mother, to look at certain out-of-the-way pictures as to which Ruskin had inspired her with a desire to see sincerely. Mrs. Tramore expressed the wish to stay at home, and the motive of this wish - a finer shade than any that even Ruskin had ever found a phrase for - was not translated into misrepresenting words by either the mother or the daughter. At San Giovanni in Bragora the girl and her companion came upon Mrs. Vaughan-Vesey, who, with one of her sisters, was also endeavouring to do the earnest thing. She did it to Rose, she did it to Captain Jay, as well as to Gianbellini; she was a handsome, long-necked, aquiline person, of a different type from the rest of her family, and she did it remarkably well. She secured our friends - it was her own expression - for luncheon, on the morrow, on the yacht, and she made it public to Rose that she would come that afternoon to invite her mother. When the girl returned to the hotel, Mrs. Tramore mentioned, before Captain Jay, who had come up to their sitting-room, that Lady Maresfield had called. "She stayed a long time - at least it seemed long!" laughed Mrs. Tramore.

The poor lady could laugh freely now; yet there was some grimness in a colloquy that she had with her daughter after Bertram Jay had departed. Before this happened Mrs. Vesey's card, scrawled over in pencil and referring to the morrow's luncheon, was brought up to Mrs. Tramore.

"They mean it all as a bribe," said the principal recipient of these civilities.

"As a bribe?" Rose repeated.

"She wants to marry you to that boy; they've seen Captain Jay and they're frightened."

"Well, dear mamma, I can't take Mr. Mangler for a husband."

"Of course not. But oughtn't we to go to the luncheon?"

"Certainly we'll go to the luncheon," Rose said; and when the affair took place, on the morrow, she could feel for the first time that she was taking her mother out. This appearance was somehow brought home to every one else, and it was really the agent of her success. For it is of the essence of this simple history that, in the first place, that success dated from Mrs. Vesey's Venetian dejeuner, and in the second reposed, by a subtle social logic, on the very anomaly that had made it dubious. There is always a chance in things, and Rose Tramore's chance was in the fact that Gwendolen Vesey was, as some one had said, awfully modern, an immense improvement on the exploded science of her mother, and capable of seeing what a "draw" there would be in the comedy, if properly brought out, of the reversed positions of Mrs. Tramore and Mrs. Tramore's diplomatic daughter. With a first-rate managerial eye she perceived that people would flock into any room - and all the more into one of hers - to see Rose bring in her dreadful mother. She treated the cream of English society to this thrilling spectacle later in the autumn, when she once more "secured" both the performers for a week at Brimble. It made a hit on the spot, the very first evening - the girl was felt to play her part so well. The rumour of the performance spread; every one wanted to see it. It was an entertainment of which, that winter in the country, and the next season in town, persons of taste desired to give their friends the freshness. The thing was to make the Tramores come late, after every one had arrived. They were engaged for a fixed hour, like the American imitator and the Patagonian contralto. Mrs. Vesey had been the first to say the girl was awfully original, but that became the general view.

Gwendolen Vesey had with her mother one of the few quarrels in which Lady Maresfield had really stood up to such an antagonist (the elder woman had to recognise in general in whose veins it was that the blood of the Manglers flowed) on account of this very circumstance of her attaching more importance to Miss Tramore's originality ("Her originality be hanged!" her ladyship had gone so far as unintelligently to exclaim) than to the prospects of the unfortunate Guy. Mrs. Vesey actually lost sight of these pressing problems in her admiration of the way the mother and the daughter, or rather the daughter and the mother (it was slightly confusing) "drew." It was Lady Maresfield's version of the case that the brazen girl (she was shockingly coarse) had treated poor Guy abominably. At any rate it was made known, just after Easter, that Miss Tramore was to be married to Captain Jay. The marriage was not to take place till the summer; but Rose felt that before this the field would practically be won. There had been some bad moments, there had been several warm corners and a certain number of cold shoulders and closed doors and stony stares; but the breach was effectually made - the rest was only a question of time. Mrs. Tramore could be trusted to keep what she had gained, and it was the dowagers, the old dragons with prominent fangs and glittering scales, whom the trick had already mainly caught. By this time there were several houses into which the liberated lady had crept alone. Her daughter had been expected with her, but they couldn't turn her out because the girl had stayed behind, and she was fast acquiring a new identity, that of a parental connection with the heroine of such a romantic story. She was at least the next best thing to her daughter, and Rose foresaw the day when she would be valued principally as a memento of one of the prettiest episodes in the annals of London. At a big official party, in June, Rose had the joy of introducing Eric to his mother. She was a little sorry it was an official party - there were some other such queer people there; but Eric called, observing the shade, the next day but one.

No observer, probably, would have been acute enough to fix exactly the moment at which the girl ceased to take out her mother and began to be taken out by her. A later phase was more distinguishable - that at which Rose forbore to inflict on her companion a duality that might become oppressive. She began to economise her force, she went only when the particular effect was required. Her marriage was delayed by the period of mourning consequent upon the death of her grandmother, who, the younger Mrs. Tramore averred, was killed by the rumour of her own new birth. She was the only one of the dragons who had not been tamed. Julia Tramore knew the truth about this - she was determined such things should not kill HER. She would live to do something - she hardly knew what. The provisions of her mother's will were published in the "Illustrated News"; from which it appeared that everything that was not to go to Eric and to Julia was to go to the fortunate Edith. Miss Tramore makes no secret of her own intentions as regards this favourite.

Edith is not pretty, but Lady Maresfield is waiting for her; she is determined Gwendolen Vesey shall not get hold of her. Mrs. Vesey however takes no interest in her at all. She is whimsical, as befits a woman of her fashion; but there are two persons she is still very fond of, the delightful Bertram Jays. The fondness of this pair, it must be added, is not wholly expended in return. They are extremely united, but their life is more domestic than might have been expected from the preliminary signs. It owes a portion of its concentration to the fact that Mrs. Tramore has now so many places to go to that she has almost no time to come to her daughter's. She is, under her son-in-law's roof, a brilliant but a rare apparition, and the other day he remarked upon the circumstance to his wife.

"If it hadn't been for you," she replied, smiling, "she might have had her regular place at our fireside."

"Good heavens, how did I prevent it?" cried Captain Jay, with all the consciousness of virtue.

"You ordered it otherwise, you goose!" And she says, in the same spirit, whenever her husband commends her (which he does, sometimes, extravagantly) for the way she launched her mother: "Nonsense, my dear - practically it was YOU!"